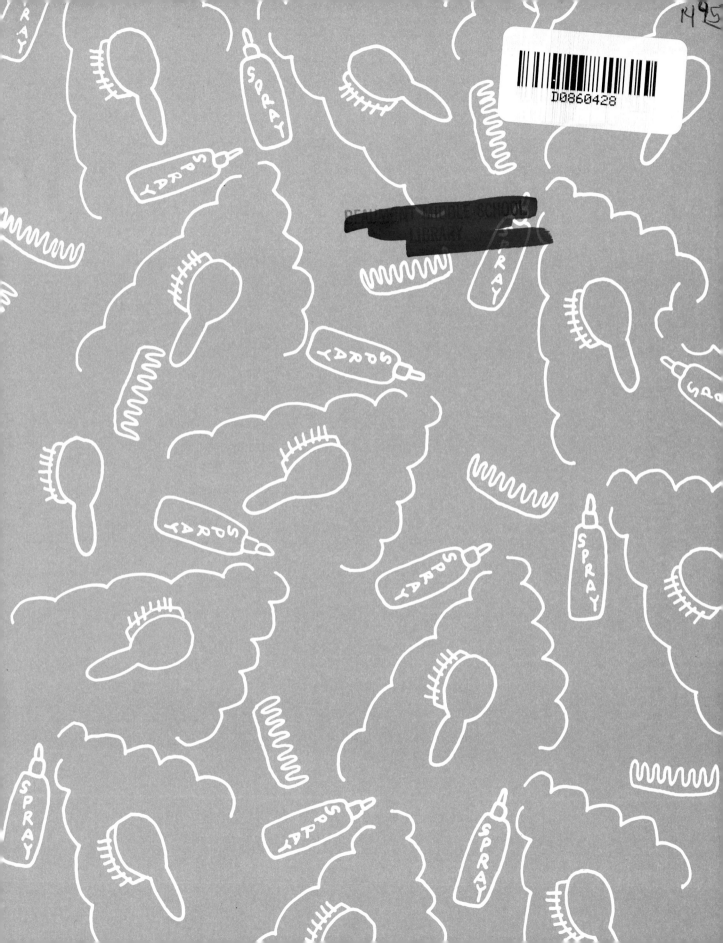

1495

D0860428

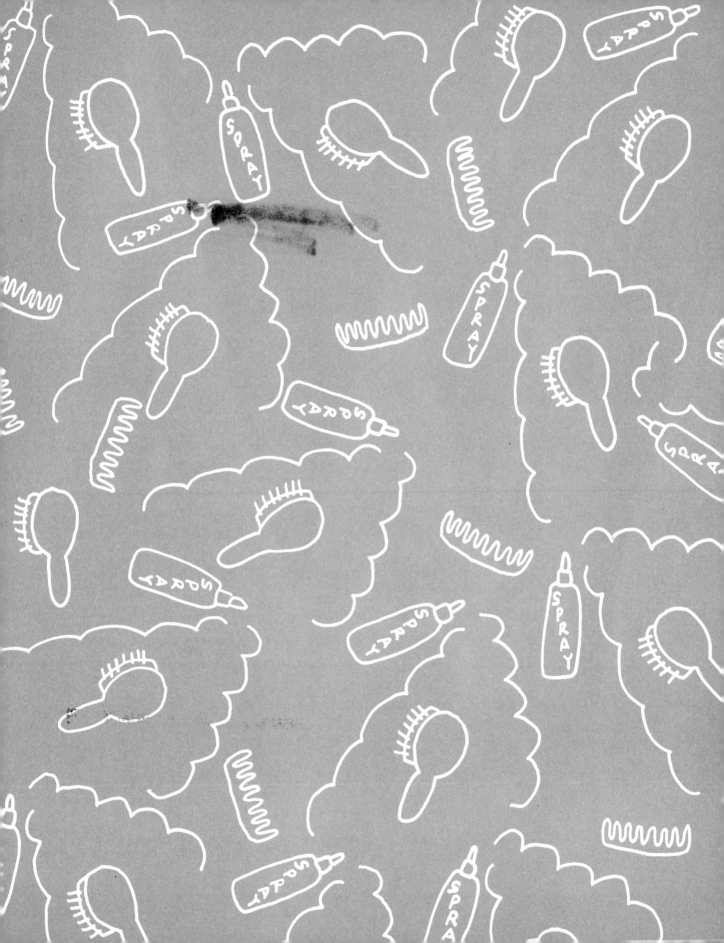

Wig!

WORDS BY the B-52's

PICTURES BY Laura Levine

Hyperion Books for Children / New York

FIRST EDITION
1 3 5 7 9 10 8 6 4 2

Library of Congress Cataloging-in-Publication Data
B-52's (Musical group)
Wig / by the B-52's ; illustrated by Laura Levine — 1st ed.
p.   cm.
Summary: Describes in pictures and words a variety of wigs and the
people who wear them. Based on a song by the B-52's.
ISBN 0-7868-0079-8 (trade) — ISBN 0-7868-2064-0 (lib. bdg.)
[1. Wigs — Fiction.   2. Hair — Fiction.]   I. Levine, Laura,
ill.   II Title.
PZ7.B1125Wi   1995
[E] — dc20   94-33486

The artwork for each picture is prepared using acrylic.

For Ricky Wilson

For Tommy

A wig!

Sally's got a *Wig.*

Ricky's got a *Wig.*

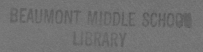

Baby's got a *wig.*

Kate's got a *wig.*

so let's go to the **neon** side of town.

Julia's got a **wig**.

Phyllis has a *wig*.

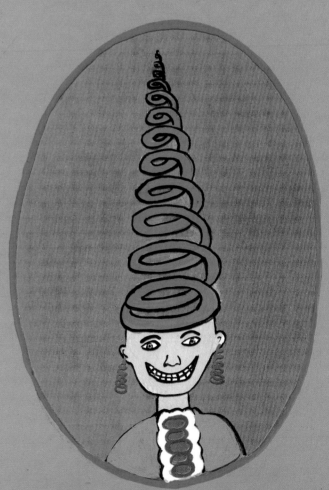

Cindy's got a *wig.*

It's got a *wig.*

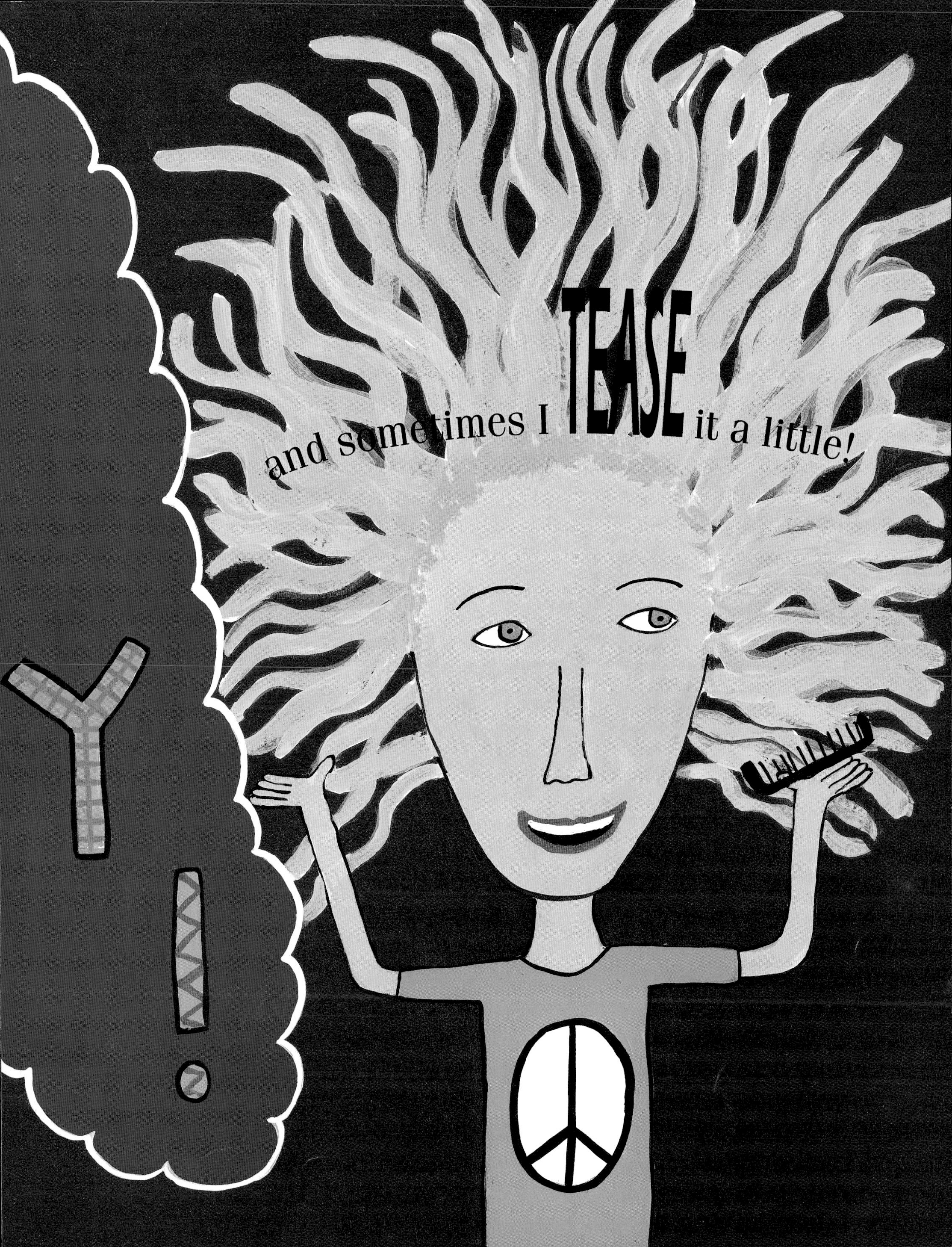
and sometimes I TEASE it a little!
Y!

. . . so let's go to the **neon** side of town.

It's 2525 . . .

START

THE
END

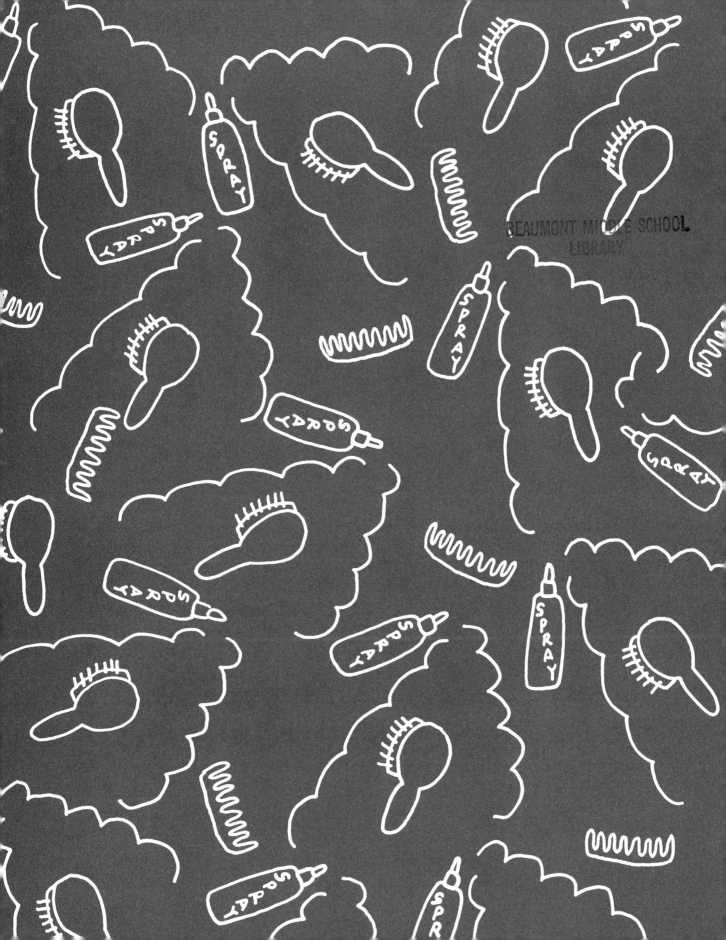